Tales from the Canyons of the Damned

Daniel Arthur Smith

Tales from the Canyons of the Damned No. 11

Tales from the Canyons of the Damned in Space No. 1

First Edition

Special thanks to Jessica West

ISBN-13: 978-0997793888 ISBN-10: 0997793880

Cover By Daniel Arthur Smith

Horror Fiction from Holt Smith ltd
Agroland
Tower

~*~

For Susan, Tristan, & Oliver, as all things are.

~*~

Flesh of My Flesh

Nathan M. Beauchamp

~*~

Behind the transparent wall of the radiation chamber, my son pulled his thighs tight against his stomach. Collin squeezed his outer eyelids closed, shutting out the distant light of the laboratory. I'd exposed him to 15,000 rads this time—twenty-fold the fatal dose for a normal human.

"Do you think he's dreaming?" my wife Magda asked. Deep wrinkles marked the corners of her eyes like river deltas.

"No, he's awake."

Her hand tightened on mine. "Hard to believe we're finally going to get to touch our little boy. Though he's not so little now."

She was right. Though only seven months old, genetic engineering had produced a child the size of a healthy two-year-old. His dense bones and powerful musculature would allow him to bear up under intense gravity. Thanks to DNA combined with genes extracted from the *Deinococcus radiodurans* bacterium, his body could repair radiation damage that would kill an unmodified human in a handful of hours. It also gave him avocado-green skin.

"I can't wait to meet him," Magda said.

The love in that voice; I turned away, brusque, focusing once again on our son. A product of an immeasurable fortune of wealth and man-hours—a body designed to survive the rocky wasteland that awaited us at the end of our long journey. The mission demanded each alteration. So why did Collin's thick-limbed body elicit in me nothing but dull fear? Shouldn't I love my progeny, regardless of its form?

"What's wrong?" Magda asked, her eyes lingering on mine.

"We've waited so long..." I tried to keep my thoughts hidden, but my face betrayed me.

"And?" Magda asked, voice sharp.

"I don't know. Leaving everything... never having any children of our own..."

"You're not going to start harping on that nonsense again, are you?"

"He's a marvel. But he's not *really* our child."

Magda turned away, shoulders tight on each side of her rigid neck, a slight flush darkening her skin. "Why don't you say what you mean? You don't love him."

Inside the chamber, Collin's foot pushed against the transparent wall, rotating to face us. His outer eyelids flicked open, closed. "He's not human," I said.

"But he's made of us! And when we reach Pericles, he'll go on to have his own children. *Your* grandchildren."

"We'll be dead by then."

"You act as if you never thought of that possibility before. We've been in flight for a half-century. You're an old man. I'm an old woman. What of it?"

How could I explain the feeling that came more and more often in the waning days of our mission? I'd read once that the Germans had a word for homesickness for a place never visited— *Fernweh*. I don't speak German but I understood. I'd never held an infant in my arms. Never heard its cries of hunger or shrieks of laughter. Never fed or bathed a child or changed a dirty diaper. No, I conducted radiation tests on my son, thermal tests, vacuum tests. And when he grew to size, Collin and the other children like him would colonize a planet I could never step foot on without a mechanized scrub suit.

"We were never meant to have children," I said, the moroseness of my words irritating even to me.

Magda whirled, face lost in a void between rage and grief. "We chose this for ourselves! Or at least I did."

I pressed my palms into my eyes and rubbed, wishing that I could retreat into the past and say something different, or even better, nothing at all.

"You're right. I'm sorry," I said. The words of an old man. A tired man.

"You just want to be left alone to wallow in self-pity."

A tone chirped from the machine. Test complete. Collin's DNA was already repairing itself, patching together chromosomes without any threat of mutation. His outer eyelids opened. Waxy nictitating membranes– protective inner eyelids expressed from vestigial DNA– slid sideways to reveal dark brown irises. What did he see, looking out at his tall, soft father? Did he fear my alien form as much as I feared his?

Collin's heart rate climbed to a steady sixty-five beats per minute. Balanced by a powerful arm, he rose to stand on his short legs. In a little less than an Earth month we would regard one another without a protective boundary separating us. I would have a choice to make. To touch or not to touch.

Looking at his strange familiar face, I searched myself for some shred of paternal feeling. Some measure of love. I found nothing. Nothing until for the first time, his eyes sparked with recognition. His chubby lips turned upward into a wide smile. Before I could stop myself, I smiled back.

~*~

The Way the World Ends
Samuel Peralta

~*~

The world will come to an end tonight.
Not with comets slanting through the rafters,

Or tidal waves surging across the coast,
Or the braze of volcanoes, unsubmerged.

Not with the earth's decimated orbit
Spiraling it into a strangled sun,

Not with the rush of spurious armies
Turning fallow the scope of mankind's dreams.

But with the last of your kiss, fading
From the sepulchre of these lips: it ends.

And the night sky may as well be shattered,
And the sun never rise again, or set,

And the stars may as well burn to cinders,
For all the worth they are, when you are gone.

~*~

Second Invasion
A.K. Meek

~*~

In the black, there was no sight, no movement, no complex thought, even though the black could only be reached by reason.

A spectacular blue light–they didn't know *blue* or *light*, for that matter–cut the black in half.

The aliens with the unpronounceable names tumbled out of the black, each gripping a pole, though they didn't know *pole*. They fell, and continued to fall, into an expanse of sky and clouds and seagulls, but it was all foreign. They were hungry as they fell.

They knew *hungry*.

The first alien invasion may have gone completely unnoticed if it wasn't for the *Carnival Breeze* that happened to be traveling back to Galveston Bay after a fun-filled nine-day excursion to the Caribbean.

Loaded down with Made in Mexico junk trinkets, the monstrous cruise ship drifted on gulf currents as a noise like a trumpet sounded, then a loud thunderclap echoed in the clear sky. In the distance, a brilliant blue appeared out of nothing, like the sky had been split by God. The blue dimmed to black and looked to be spitting up coffee grounds into the gulf. But as passengers pinch-zoomed in on their cells, grainy resolution showed it wasn't coffee grounds at all, but bodies.

For ten minutes, two-thousand Carnival passengers were treated to more than any of them had anticipated when they booked their $792-per-person rooms. Hundreds of bodies fell into the water, never to surface again.

A month later, once the nation's interest had worn thin with the "end of the world" storyline and everyone had moved on to the next social cataclysm, Bob Skinner, an intrepid fisherman, set out from Galveston Bay to where the cruise ship had seen the bodies sink. Countless sharks and scavenger fish still crowded the area, and Bob landed a hammerhead for the record books.

So ended the first invasion.

~*~

Never one to waste another precious moment, Trisha Waring burned through her fifteen minutes of fame in seven.

Coming out of the worst summer of her life, she had decided to take a cruise to clear her head and reevaluate life. She was one of 2,000 to see the rift in the sky.

Shortly after, she had been contacted to appear on a local conspiracy theory/UFO podcast for a few hundred dollars. It was enough for her to take her two kids on a day trip to downtown San Antonio, maybe do some shopping, definitely stop for lunch at the Rainforest Café. The Mahi Mahi platter was the best.

Daniel worked close to the café, a couple of blocks away, but that was beside the point.

As she and her two sons exited the parking garage,

heading to the downtown tourist district, Davey tugged on his mother's sleeve. "Mom," he whined in his best eight-year-old whiny voice, "can we go on the boats? Or the Alamo?"

Daniel Jr., named after his father, shook his head in utter twelve-year-old disgust and took a cheap swipe at his brother's skinny arm. "Forget the boats. Those are for babies. Let's go to the Alamo." He aimed an imaginary longrifle, fired, and hit one of Santa Anna's men square between the eyes.

"We've seen it a hundred times," Trisha said, brushing away a new shock of purple-streaked bangs in her otherwise dishwater blond hair. She had dyed it in the hope of possibly stealing back some of her youth, some of the moments she had wasted on her husband. Her hair was a purple elixir to reverse the spread of time, number five on an alchemist's bucket list of potions to create. "Come on you two." She motioned to a set of wrought iron stairs leading from surface streets down to the Riverwalk. She guided her boys through the flow of gawking tourists shuffling from one novelty shop or restaurant to the next.

A trumpet blast erupted. Some of the musically-inclined tourists stopped in place, thinking it an unusual note struck for a mariachi band. But for Trisha, a chill ran through her as thoughts of the cruise she had been on six months ago came flooding back.

A thunderclap split the clear sky.

Davey continued tugging on his mother. "What's that? Is it a carnival?"

She ignored him and stared at the sky, which was a pale watercolor aquamarine. White cotton clouds bloomed in daytime heat. She breathed a sigh as she didn't see what she expected to see, but then gulped when she saw what she didn't want to see.

With a brilliant blue, the sky split in half, exposing a distant black. Then a body fell out. Trisha and her boys, and thousands of Texans and tourists, watched it fall.

It was like a skydiver streaking from the heavens, but it had no parachute. It continued on its descent until it reached the building tops and clipped one. That collision appeared to have severed a section of it, as two chunks went spinning wildly in opposite directions, getting lost in the San Antonio skyline.

Then a hundred more bodies fell from the rift.

~*~

"Sounds like rain," Daniel said as the thunderclap faded to memory. Moments later, the sound of a trumpet rippled, but he figured it was just the building acoustics. He and his colleagues sat at a meeting table on the upper floor of the Hyatt Regency, in the business suites. Strewn across the table were papers scribbled with notes, memory joggers, and mind maps. An explosion of productivity and corporate sprawl. His eyes lingered on Tina, the new quality manager.

She glanced up at the ceiling as she playfully ran her fingers through her hair, then screamed as the first body slammed into the glass skylight that ran the length of the corporate meeting room. The second and third bodies spidered the tempered glass. The fourth caved it in.

Slabs of shattered ceiling rained, a grim nightmare storm as hulking bodies–more or less human-shaped, but larger and colored a dirty charcoal, with tufts of wire, maybe hair, covering them in random spots–tumbled through the opening. They crashed to the floor, spurting green goo where dagger glass shards shredded their disgusting bodies.

The business meeting broke up, everyone scattering in

a mad panic except for Tina. A massive windowpane, roughly the size of a Whirlpool refrigerator, landed on Daniel's mid-life girlfriend.

His legs didn't work like he expected, his mind occupied, wrenched with incredulity. The strange, impossible bodies, his girlfriend being crushed in a rain of glass. The horror of it all.

Then he thought about his family, wondered where his estranged wife and kids were.

~*~

One alien rifted in not far above the Hyatt's business suites, plopping into the meeting room relatively unscathed. It stood on what could be considered its legs. It held a pole.

And as an ant mindlessly drones about the day, feeding, storing, fighting, with no thought of purpose, only propelled by sheer instinct, so the alien with the unpronounceable name leveled its pole at Daniel and fired.

The pent up anguish of countless memories consumed but forgotten struck him full in the chest, knocking him to the floor. The bullet of misery didn't damage the body, but shredded the mind.

Daniel shrieked as the unfathomable cleaved his sanity. He ripped at the paisley tie wrapped around his neck. Leaping to his feet, he ran headlong and through a thin glass wall partitioning the room in half, creating a symphony of crystal piano keys.

The alien didn't see the resulting gore of countless grievous lacerations Daniel received as a reward for shattering the glass wall with his body, but grape clouds blooming from the wounds. A tasty cloud of dying fear covered Daniel before he even hit the floor.

The alien rushed over to his fallen body and pushed

what might be considered its face into the cloud. If it had lungs, it would have breathed deeply, but it didn't need to.

It absorbed the cloud, the memory fog, as it rolled over rigid folds of skin, sweeping across hair-like protrusions, each bristle drinking in Daniel's thoughts as water.

And the horrible alien then understood the businessman's irrational, mind-bending, terror-drenched dying thoughts that composed the cloud.

It learned of his *fear*–it liked that word–of watching his girlfriend crushed.

It digested paralyzing *revulsion* and *incomprehension*. Both also good words.

The cloud fed the alien, feeding its hunger. Yes, *feeding hunger*. That's always... *good*. It understood the... *human*, human mind breaking at the *alien invasion*.

Alien invasion sounded about right.

The alien satisfyingly sipped the last of Daniel's thoughts into itself, and the very last thought on the human's mind before the... pole—yes, *pole-weapon*, pole-weapon drove him insane was the human's mate. And mate-offspring.

If the alien had a human mouth with lips, it would have smiled in satisfaction.

~*~

The San Antonio streets had erupted in chaos.

The city dispersed as aliens appeared at varying heights, some in the clouds, some only a couple feet off the ground. But gravity was still at work and commanded them all. Many slammed to the earth, never to rise. But some lived through the hard landings, and that was enough.

Each carried a pole, and each bullet of misery unleashed another horror. Men went insane. Men turned on men. Men died.

Trisha had to stop to catch her breath. Ever since her chemo protocol ended last year, her stamina had sucked. Instead of catching her breath, she wanted to scream, to curl into a ball and wish it all away. She wanted her husband there with her. But she didn't. She couldn't.

Fear, no, excruciating fright, could be a great motivator.

She gulped one more time–the moist air doing nothing to ease her burning throat–and tightened her mother-grip on her youngest kid's arm. "Davey, come on."

In the distance, metal crunched; an accident. A car horn sounded and didn't stop.

A man ran through the panicked crowd. He hollered like a maniac as he ripped his own hair out. He swung at others as they passed.

A woman, an older lady in a flower print moo moo, lunged at a teenager too slow to avoid her. She grabbed hold of the teenager's long black hair and dragged her to the ground, stomped on her neck. No one stopped to help. Trisha wasn't about to stop and risk the lives of her children.

An alien shuffled from a Walgreens, sending a wave of screams through the streets. Without concern for the surrounding chaos, the alien pointed its pole-weapon at a business woman in high heels and a tight skirt who had tripped over a curb.

She screamed a death scream, spasmed, and abruptly stopped jerking, her body contorted. The alien rushed to tower over her then swayed back and forth, like it was meditating or moving to some unheard music.

That horrified Trisha more than seeing the business woman die of fright.

She dragged her kids, both of them now crying for

their father, maneuvering them through the mass. Each frantic person believed their chosen escape route would lead them away from the horror.

Two more of the appalling alien invaders materialized out of nothing, about fifteen feet away from Trisha, and dropped. One landed on a set of sidewalk café patio furniture, which sent pieces flying. The second plopped on top of iron railing surrounding the patio. The railing easily crumpled under the tall hulking body, but in the process the alien got tangled in a nest of metal, pinning it to the ground. The horrible beast struggled to break free.

A teenager, eighteen and foolish enough to be wearing all black during a south Texas summer, broke from the stampede and snatched the pole from the alien trapped in the nest. He disappeared back into the crowd.

Trisha's side stitched. She couldn't take a solid breath as her lungs burned. "Hurry," she gasped to her kids, as if they needed to be reminded.

One wild man, wearing a policeman's uniform, ripped a baby from its mother's arms. Before he could do anything with the precious cargo, another man, a biker with a beer belly and his beard in a braid, ran up behind the policeman and grabbed him in a head lock. They fought.

The world was falling apart around her. If only her husband was here. If only he hadn't walked out on her and their children. She cursed his name.

She had spent so many years, fifteen total, supporting him. Sacrificing her dreams of teaching, giving it all up for him despite what her mother had said. She spent two months of sleepless nights, praying for him, tending to his every whim, as they waited for the blood tests to come back, to see if he needed further treatment for the melanoma etched across his shoulders. Fortunately,

Doctor Baker had given him a clean bill of health.

They traded cancer stories.

But he had forgotten her appointment when she found out she had breast cancer. She had to rely on Nancy, a neighbor she'd talked to a handful of times, to get her to weekly treatments. He had important client meetings that kept him from staying home when she was too tired to make dinner. If he would have missed the meetings it would have cost millions, so he said.

She had told herself repeatedly it wasn't because he didn't care. He was being a good husband, providing for his family.

The worst kind of lies are those you tell yourself for so long you convince yourself they're true. After fifteen years, it became Trisha's hard lesson.

A woman bumped into Trisha and they both came to a dead stop. "Where are you going?" the lady said, her eyes distracted, like she was late for an appointment and inconvenienced by the encounter.

Trisha shook her head. "I'm..." Truth was she had never thought about where to run, only that she needed to run hard and run fast. "I'm not sure."

"The Alamo," the lady said before she bolted away. "Remember the Alamo," she yelled over her shoulder. She disappeared around a building corner.

Trisha thought about it, turning the idea over. Up until this moment, since the beginning of the worst summer of her life, she had been on autopilot. Now she realized where her subconscious, her inner her, had been leading her and her two boys.

They stood in front of the Hyatt, where her husband of fifteen years worked. The same husband that announced at dinner, Taco Bell Tuesday, two months ago, that he needed to find himself.

No, she didn't need to go there. He couldn't do anything else for her. Or her kids.

Maybe it was growing up in the Texas public education system, when Texas history was more important than American. The crux of the republic's existence was painted with the glory of thirteen days, when the independent spirit held back over fifteen hundred.

She needed to get to the Alamo. Others would be there. They'd be fine.

"Come on!" She almost jerked poor Davey's skinny arm out of its socket as she yanked him along. Daniel stayed on her heels. "We're going to the Alamo," she said with determined finality.

~*~

Such strange and odd thoughts filled humans' heads as they breathed their last.

The alien with the unpronounceable name mulled over sitting at seat A-4, First Class, waiting for the MD-11 to back away from its parking ramp. It wondered why the "wheels on the bus go round and round." It considered whether Van Halen was better off with Sammy Hagar than David Lee Roth.

It had become drunk on human thought, memories that flowed from owners who no longer needed them. They were left as empty... *husks*. Yes, that. Not corn husks. Human husks. It was a figure of speech.

As fulfilling as the buffet of thoughts were, there was nothing quite like that first one.

The alien smacked its foul mouth, remembering Daniel as it made its way to the building's exit. A human, its very essence spent, propped the Hyatt's entrance door open. It stepped over the thoughtless body.

It was on a *road*—no, *street*. Yes, that. Many more

humans had fallen on the street like... like... *daisies* in a garden. A human garden of daisies, except they were all wilted.

Others of its kind were about, scouring the humans, searching for any last stray thought hidden in a folded sleeve or pants leg. *Clothes.* They prodded the bodies with their horrible, insanity-inducing pole-weapons. Many of its kind had also fallen.

It shuffled along the street, the south Texas sun beating down on strange flesh that never should have set foot on earth. Screams and fighting and death drew it, the alien sensing an abundance of thoughts in one direction.

Pausing, it turned its head upward.

Up there was the rift of velvet-black leading back to its home world. Foreign, distant stars twinkled in the tear in daytime. For a moment, the shambling mess of illogic stared at the rip in reason. What almost passed as homesickness or nostalgia swept across its mind.

Then the chaos of a society collapsing pulled its attention from the rift. Hunger typically drove its desire, but it was more than hunger now; it was a remembrance. Daniel's mate and the mate-offspring were near. So near it could taste them on its arm.

The alien lumbered down the street, following the remnants of the Waring family.

~*~

They sidestepped bodies frozen in horrid positions, twisted in unspeakable manners. Who knew how they died.

Fights had broken out as man killed man, driven to rage by the pole-weapons.

Dark heads bobbed over the madness; black shepherds to insane sheep.

Every turn Trisha made, she found fewer and fewer

people. At some point, the dead started to outnumber the alive, strewn human bodies mingled with alien.

It was chaotic and horrible. It was humanity falling apart; life coming to a sudden end in the worst way possible. The end of an age. That's what Trisha was seeing. It wasn't supposed to end like this. Getting mowed down by aliens with sticks wasn't a way the scientists and philosophers said it would all end. But enough retrospective mourning, she needed to focus on getting her kids to safety, to the Alamo.

She found a stairway that led from the surface streets down to the Riverwalk, to Mexican restaurants, sports bars, trinket shops, and tattoo parlors.

Here and there, from behind locked storefront doors, people scoped the surroundings, then secreted themselves back into their hiding spots.

A business man emerged from a thin alley, both arms wrapped tightly around a bundle, probably a baby. His head darted left to right to left, like in that moment he had to make a decision which could mean life or death for him and his child.

It very well could.

Trisha understood that feeling, that weighty decision when the life of your loved ones depended on one simple decision. But then that made the decision not so simple, after all.

Gunshots echoed in the distance, off the shops, the alleys, the water. And screaming. But the direction couldn't be determined. The fighting was everywhere.

As they neared the Alamo, the gunshots grew louder. There was a large commotion in front and tall alien bodies were at the center.

Fearful they'd be seen, Trisha guided her boys to a patio café sun umbrella, red and green and yellow, knocked to its side and pushed against a wall. They ducked behind the temporary cover.

Yards from the Alamo, the smallish, brown stone monument to a state, was where many others had obviously decided to find safety.

~*~

Humans fell, humans screamed, humans attacked humans with a viciousness brought about by insanity. With bare hands, they ripped at each other. The aliens and their pole-weapons brought out the anger and hate always resting just beneath the surface.

If the alien had known the purpose of a smile, it would've strained to force its revolting orifice to comply. But it did know *enjoy*, having just absorbed it from the mate-offspring celebrating its tenth birthday. *Tenth* is a number, after *ninth*. Like *two*. *Twoth? No, second*.

Two humans stood in front of the building called the *Alamo*. It knew this building well. The alien had become bloated on all the thoughts it had drunk of the Alamo. The first had been Ted, who died as he ran a utensil through his own throat. The alien considered *utensil. Fork* was more appropriate. Ted thought of the Alamo and if a mate called *Esmeralda* had made it.

But Ted's thoughts weren't as satisfying as the thoughts of people who died in anger, when they killed friends and family in fits of manufactured rage. That's what got the juices flowing. Men didn't need much prompting to turn on one another. A mind-bending, impossible bullet often did the trick.

Ted's thoughts were *bland*, as Chef Garcia–the woman whose memories the alien absorbed minutes before Ted– would've said. Chef Garcia had also taught the alien *sweet*, *savory*, and *sour*. The alien rationalized that Ted, who ran a fork through his neck, could've used a pinch of fury.

Maybe then his thoughts wouldn't have been so bland.

Like a Thanksgiving turkey with extra stuffing. But not too much clove. Drool dripped from the alien's unholy orifice as it pondered all the remembrances it had eaten over the past hour.

But it was still hungry.

Its strange eyes focused on the Alamo. The Alamo was... *sane... surely...* no, *safe*. Yes, that. But not for long.

The two humans in front of the Alamo aimed weapons, fired. The alien thought of *thunder* as an appropriate word. Thunder sounded as humans, male and female, cracked shots off.

One of its kind–hovering over a man, drinking in his thoughts that flowed from his head in rainbow hues–was struck by the thunder. It gave an otherworldly shriek and fell backwards to the street, jerking like squid tentacles frying in a vat of bubbling oil. *Calamari.*

Protocol allowed another one of its kind, the closest, to shuffle to the human with the rainbow thoughts and finish the meal. But the alien needed to stop the thunder.

It fired its pole-weapon at the male, hitting him in the stomach. He staggered, screamed, slapped himself in the face. Turning his weapon to the female, he pressed the trigger but it didn't thunder. He yelled and threw it at her. She gasped at her husband who had suddenly turned evil then sprinted for the Alamo.

Another male near the Alamo entrance pointed his pole-weapon at the enraged man, and one thunder dropped him. Lime green and slate gray streaked from his chest.

The alien claimed dibs, moved to the man, and drank the muddy green thoughts erupting from him and remembered when he got his first job, right out of college. An entry level programmer. It turned the word *programmer* over in its mind.

It stopped its swaying as a familiar sensation crept up its morbid spine. *Family*, it thought.

Turning, it lumbered toward an... *object* colored red and green and yellow. Colored like thoughts, but not quite. The object leaned against a building. Not the Alamo building.

It sensed third humans. Wait, no... *three*. It sensed three humans behind the object.

The sky shimmered in strange electric gloss-black. The rift that brought the aliens led to a place beyond human logic and understanding. It led to a *reasoning*. It couldn't be found by travel or by human vehicle. The alien home world wasn't a planet; it could only be reached through a state of reason.

This strange earth, this strange land bursting with alien humans were ripe... *fruit*, ready to be plucked. And eaten. With a hint of lime to bring out the flavor.

With its pole-weapon, it gently moved the object aside and recognized Daniel's mate and mate-offspring.

And in an odd and inexplicable circumstance, the alien with the unpronounceable name reunited the Waring family.

~*~

The Peacemaker
Kevin Lauderdale

~*~

The view from the balcony was lovely until it exploded. Faster than he had time to realize what was happening, he fell from the second story.

The air was thick with dust and smoke. Moab Wintner did his best to wave it away between coughs. Slowly, he propped himself up on one side to survey the damage. He was surrounded by fist-sized chunks of the green-veined, white marble that had been the balcony, and by singed strands of rattan that had been the furniture. At least all the rubble was beneath him. Wintner was sore all over, and there were a few lacerations on his arms and chest, but he was still alive. He hadn't known marble could splinter like that. There was a lot of it. The large balcony had been about the same size as the bridge of his orbiting command ship.

A strong wind blew through, parting the smoke like curtains and revealing the rest of the plaza.

"May Sabu take the eyes of the Troth!" yelled First Speaker Fen'ra as he crawled over the wreckage towards Wintner. His clothes were torn and scorched, and there were streaks of cobalt blue blood on his face, emphasizing the elongated, almost horse-like head of the otherwise humanoid Menimian. "Are you seriously injured, Ambassador?"

Wintner carefully moved into a sitting position and flexed his arms, legs, back, and neck. "Nothing broken." He turned his head and looked up. The explosion had destroyed only the semi-circular balcony that had once jutted from the Municpal Building. The hole in the wall gaped like the black mouth of a giant.

Wintner said, "I take it that was a bomb of some sort."

Fen'ra nodded. "Troth, as I'd mentioned before. When they can't do something big, they do something small. They don't care, so long as they destroy."

More Menimians streamed out from the street-level doors of the building and towards the rubble. A handful were Cintro security guards in their yellow and grey camouflage fatigues.

"We're fine," said Fen'ra, waving them away. "Secure the area."

Second Speaker Gulta, who had only just stepped out onto the balcony a moment before the explosion, hobbled up.

"They failed!" Gulta cried. "No one was killed." The flannel of his face, pinto white-and-brown, was also streaked with blue blood. His uniform was torn and smoky, but he had fared better than Wintner or the First Speaker. "What do you think? A mortar attack? Not a grenade. We were too high up."

Wintner shook his head. "I didn't see anyone down there." True, he hadn't been looking straight down all the time. Fen'ra and Gulta had taken him out to view the sunset. The way the light from Menim's sun first refracted on the glass of the buildings and then colored the creamy stone of the plaza had been stunning, spreading shifting rainbows for a kilometer at least. "It had to have been an explosive device planted on the balcony," he said.

"It must have been small to be so easily concealed," Fen'ra said. "That would account for the fact that the explosion didn't kill us, but only blew away the balcony."

Gulta picked up a piece of the shattered marble. "The only entrance to that balcony was under guard for a complete miron before we arrived."

"Then they must have sneaked the explosive onto the balcony prior to the guard's arrival."

Wintner looked back up at the hole. "There wasn't much on the balcony. Where exactly did they hide it?"

"Perhaps in a dalma plant."

Now that Wintner thought about it, he vaguely recalled seeing two unobtrusive little trees, about his height, on either side of the balcony. They were the sort of decorating afterthoughts you might see at any government facility on any planet. Completely unremarkable, and so practically invisible.

Fen'ra gestured away from the rubble. "Come, Ambassador. You will need some dermal work. If you prefer to return to your ship, we understand, but I will tell you with pride that Menimian tiamat root works wonders on minor muscle damage."

"Root will be fine." Wintner was already feeling better, but it never hurt to appease the natives a little; let their witch doctors give you an herb, sip the local fermented beverage… He looked up again at the hole. *The universe is filled with violence and chaos*, his instructors at the War College always said. *It is the role of peacemakers to force order upon that chaos.*

The First Speaker scratched his head. "Someone knew when we would be on that balcony."

Gulta said, "Access to the Ambassador's itinerary was kept under multiple-encryption."

Fen'ra's small ears stood up, something Wintner now recognized as a sign of anger. "Obviously, the Troth have found a way to defeat your vaunted security system. Order all of the passwords changed. Immediately!"

"Yes, First Speaker!" replied Gulta, who set off back toward the Municipal Building's main entrance with a limp. Two of the guards tried to help him, but he shrugged them away. "More Troth atrocities," he muttered, hurling the piece of marble to the ground.

~*~

"They sting us and sting us, like so many little salli flies," said Gulta. "And all we do in return is swat at them."

Wintner rubbed the muscles on his right forearm. He had to admit that the tiamat root had done wonders for his skin, but his muscles were still sore.

They were sitting in the First Speaker's office. It was located at the opposite end of the building from where the balcony had been. His desk, like the chairs Wintner and Gulta sat on, was made from the honey-colored rattan that was so abundant on Menim. There were no dalma plants.

"They bomb our fuel pipelines," the Second Speaker continued, "and we impose trade embargoes. They hijack our ships, and we negotiate. They attempt to assassinate a Coalition ambassador"–he looked pointedly at Wintner–"and we swat at them. Correction: we have yet to retaliate for that. But when we do, it will be a mere swat." He stood up. "We need to strike harder, First Speaker! We have the power. We can eradicate them once and for all. And then we will have peace."

Fen'ra rubbed his temples. This was obviously not the first time he had heard these arguments.

Slowly, patiently, Fen'ra said, "We have it. But we must not use it." He turned to Wintner. "We Cintro are the only nation-state on Menim to possess nuclear weapons." He smiled. "I imagine your Coalition is beyond crude fission."

"What good is it," demanded Gulta, "to possess it if we never use it?"

"We cannot use it because that is not who we are. We are not destroyers. We are builders. We are not slaughterers, we are healers." Fen'ra sighed. "But, we have it...and you cannot put the seeds back into a rella plant."

Gulta asked, "How does the Coalition deal with such things, Ambassador?"

Wintner paused. He was on Menim at the First Speaker's invitation to "put a human face" (so to speak) on the Coalition. Menim had made contact with the Coalition via radio telescope a decade ago. It was only after much dialog that now an ambassador had been sent. He was there to answer questions about the Coalition with an eye toward Menim possibly becoming a member.

"In order to join the Coalition," he said, "a planet must have a unified, world-wide government."

"Are there no guerilla factions?" asked Gulta. "No one on *any* Coalition planet who opposes that government and strikes against it?"

"Such grievances may be addressed by Coalition facilitators or the Coalition Council, if warranted." Fen'ra looked impressed. Perhaps too impressed. Wintner hastened to add, "Not that life in the Coalition is a paradise. People, no matter what planet they're from, being people, there will always be some fighting. But we keep striving, we keep working for greater harmony. That is what the Coalition is all about."

Fen'ra nodded. "Well, it is starting to look like we will never be unified enough to join the Coalition. Other nation-states have allied with us, but still others insist on their own ways."

"Something," said Wintner, "that must be respected."

"Cintro is not an empire, Ambassador. We are quite content to allow other nations to go their own way. If they want to be left alone—"

"Self-isolated," said Gulta.

"—then we respect their wishes. Perhaps they will come around in time. But when other nations attack us, striking at us for ideological reasons, we cannot ignore them. Small as Troth is, it strikes at us over and again." He sighed. "It's actually quite remarkable that a nation barely the size of our largest shire is able to gather the resources to launch these attacks. They have practically nothing. They are poor and largely uneducated. It's amazing that they can accomplish anything despite their poverty."

"Perhaps it's the other way around," said Gulta. "Their poverty is caused by their 'accomplishments.' All their resources are channeled towards our destruction. Naturally, they don't have much left over to provide for their cit—I almost said 'citizens.' But they aren't citizens. Their *subjects*."

"And what have we done to deserve this, Ambassador? We exist. Our mere presence is an affront to them."

"Are you officially at war?" asked Wintner. "That would preclude membership in the Coalition."

Gulta laughed hollowly. "It's a bit of a one-sided war, Ambassador. They consider us the source of all evil on our world, and they strike at us over and over again in these tiny—though occasionally deadly—attacks. We, on the other hand, try to engage them constructively. When that fails—and it always fails—we engage in extremely measured responses."

To Wintner, Fen'ra said, "Too measured, Gulta thinks."

Gulta said, "They destroyed an air transport with one hundred people onboard. Mostly Cintro, but some Saund, and a few Desterian tourists as well. Our response was to destroy one of their solturium facilities."

"Because they used solturium," added Fen'ra, "in making the explosive. We destroyed it in the middle of the night, when it was unoccupied, so that we wouldn't hurt anyone."

"An appropriate, and, indeed, measured response," said Wintner.

Gulta said, "We should have killed one hundred of their people."

"One hundred innocent civilians, Gulta?" asked Fen'ra.

"No more innocent than the people on our transport. Besides, one hundred for one hundred is a perfect equation."

"On my planet," said Wintner, "we have an ancient saying: 'An eye for an eye eventually blinds the whole world.'"

Gulta frowned. "Measured responses have yet to put an end to their terrorist activities. They keep coming back. Sometimes it's remote bombs, like today. Sometimes it's suicidal assassins who walk into market crowds and detonate themselves. You never know where they will turn up or what they will do next. It's rarely the same thing twice."

"And are you the source of all evil, First Speaker?" asked Wintner.

Fen'ra laughed. "I hope not. We are a constitutional republic with full suffrage." He turned to the Second Speaker, "Gulta, are we evil?"

"Evil would not try," said Gulta through clenched teeth.

"And we have tried. Over and over. They will not listen. Perhaps if one of their cities were to vanish in a nuclear flash then they would listen."

"At least they have stopped assassinating our envoys," said Fen'ra. "When we communicate, it starts reasonably, but they soon shout us down with wholesale condemnations of our politics, our forms of entertainment, our tolerance for…Oh, it is very difficult to have meaningful negations with someone who is convinced that you are Sabu herself."

Wintner asked, "Have you tried negotiation with different representatives of Troth?"

"There are no others," said Fen'ra.

Wintner nodded. Menim had to have a single world-government. The Coalition was composed of planets, not nation-states. Anything smaller simply did not work on a galactic scale.

There was a loud buzzing noise outside. Gulta turned and started to yell, but his voice was drowned out by the sound of shattering glass. Three steel-grey ropes shot through the window and wrapped themselves around Wintner: one around his legs, one his arms and chest, and a third around his neck. With one crude jerk, they pulled him though the jagged window and out into the night sky.

Wintner saw some sort of crude flying machine above him. Barely large enough to hold its pilot, it had four wings and trailed white smoke. The ropes projected themselves from the thing's undercarriage. The angry red light of Cintro energy weapons shot from the ground up at the machine. Wintner could feel their heat as the blasts passed near him. The machine rocked.

For the second time that day, he fell.

~*~

"Welcome to Troth, Ambassador," said a Menimian wearing a brown uniform and pointing a blaster at his face. The slightly higher tone to the voice and the broader head indicated this was a female.

Wintner was lying on the floor of a cave. He shook his head

to clear his mind. The aircraft must have righted itself, and he must have passed out.

Troth. So, he had been kidnapped. Crude, but effective. Troth was an island not too far away from Cintro's continent. They must have drawn him up into the flying machine or transferred him to a boat while he was unconscious. He could not have spent hours of travel time dangling from those ropes.

"Up!" demanded the Troth. She gestured to her left. "Go!"

Wintner was even more sore now, but he was able to walk. The cave was illuminated by waist-high cylinders running on small batteries, but a shaft of natural light leaked through an opening in the stone wall at head-height. Outside, it was morning. Through the crack, he glanced at a city of squat, low buildings made of what he recognized as the Menimian equivalent of concrete.

A sharp weapon prodded Wintner in the back. "Keep moving."

They passed by a large cavern where a flying machine lay strewn about in sections. A Menimian standing near it held a piece up to the light for a moment, then, with a digusted grunt, let it drop to the ground. The craft had made it back, but, apparently, just barely.

No wonder the Troth struck in so many different ways; they lacked the resources (or the ability) to build anything reusable. Gulta had said they were poor. They probably put everything they had at the time into one attack, then pieced the next one together starting from scratch.

The woman with the gun steered Wintner to a smaller room in the cave. "General Ejar," she said.

A Menimian with streaks of grey on his face sat behind a desk. Aside from the construction materials, Ejar's office wasn't that different from First Speaker Fen'ra's. There was a red and yellow flag (the Troth colors, Wintner assumed), chairs, and a desk. But Ejar's furniture seemed to be carved from stone. The woman pointed with her gun at a chair. It was hard, but Wintner found it quite supportive and generally comfortable when he sat. The Troth were obviously extremely resourceful.

General Ejar said, "Ambassador Wintner, I take it. This is a great victory for us. I've been watching the vids." He stood up and walked around the desk. "A representative of the great Coalition! A mighty interstellar force! And tiny us. We captured you." He picked up a small, sand-colored stone and contemplated it. "Who is more mighty? The giant, or the grell-ant who fells him? I hope you have learned a lesson in humility." He squeezed his fist and the stone crumbled to dust. "But I doubt it."

"The Coalition has no argument with Troth, General. I'm here to talk about your planet joining—"

"You are working with the Cintro! Perhaps I will simply kill you. I know how much you people value your lives. That's why you make such ineffective soldiers. Your own life must mean nothing or you cannot prevail."

Winter said, "Prevailing means nothing to me if I am not around to see it. That's why peacemakers are cautious. Perhaps you do not want to see the world you are making. That's why you're happy to kill yourselves."

Keep them talking. If he could reason with them, that would be best. He had a back-up plan. It had worked before with the Bamse, but he really didn't want to use it. It was purely a last-ditch solution, and far from fool-proof.

Ejar sat down again. "Immaterial. I am going to trade you for a fission bomb."

"The Cintro won't trade anything for me. I'm not one of them. I'm not even a Meminian."

"They will trade for you. They need you. Your loss would be catastrophic. They are so desperate to join the Coalition. Then the friendly aliens will descend from the clouds and solve all of our problems. Ha! You weren't even safe in an office building. Alliance with you will get us nowhere."

"What exactly is your disagreement with the Cintro?"

"They are the only nation on this planet with such weapons. They feel free to dictate morals and politics throughout the entire world because they can enforce them."

"But," said Wintner, "they do not. I have seen no evidence of coercion."

"No, they are much more subtle than that. They don't openly say, 'Become a republic or we will destroy you. Allow this or that or we will destroy you.' We are not a republic. We were not meant to be one. It is not our way."

"Not your way?" asked Wintner. "Not your way to let people have a say in their own government?"

"People cannot govern themselves. They are far too foolish, too easily swayed. You have met the leaders of Cintro. So handsome, so well-spoken. Not very clever. And, oh, so decadent. Little wonder they turned to nuclear forces. That way the cowards can kill from a distance."

"But," said Wintner, "once you have the same armaments, what does that make you?"

"We need them purely as a deterrent! They would not dare strike us if they know we can retaliate."

"But you strike them all the time, and they don't retaliate."

"They are fools as well as cowards," said Ejar. "We would not hesitate so."

"General!" A red-streaked female stuck her head around the corner. "News from Cintro. We activated one of our agents. He met with the First Speaker about the trade. They turned us down, of course, and then they let him go!"

Ejar laughed. "They had one of our agents in the room with them, and they let him go. What fools! How do they ever manage to rule the world?" To Wintner, he said, "It was always only the slimmest of chances that Fen'ra would give up weapons in exchange for you." He produced a blaster from its holster at his side and pointed it at Wintner. "Which is why now *you* will provide us with weapons if you want to live."

There was only one way out. Just like with the Bamse. He hated to do it, but an ambassador was only as good as his acting skills. Sometimes you had to fake ignorance or indifference. Sometimes you had to fake moral rectitude. Sometimes you had to fake bravery.

And sometimes you had to fake fear.

"Um…" Wintner darted his eyes around. That always made for a good show. "You know… The Coalition doesn't owe this planet anything. What do we care if you have a bomb or not." He intentionally slowed down, as if just realizing something. "In fact…it would balance things, wouldn't it? Yes. There has to be peace in order for the Coalition to take a serious look here."

"Now you are making sense," said Ejar with a smile.

"Yes, I think I could see how this would work."

"Of course. Balance it out." The General spread his arms in largess. "Let us all be reasonable."

Wintner added, "And once we have balance, perhaps then you can be unified."

"Of course," the General said with a smile. "Once everyone is equal, then there's nothing to fight over. Unity is guaranteed." But his smile was much too broad to be real. Apparently, the General knew how to fake things as well.

~*~

The Coalition astroplane slowly descended towards them. Wintner, the General, and about a hundred Troth stood in a circle around the huge granite courtyard in the middle of the city. The low buildings of Troth radiated out in all directions from there.

Several Troth kept their weapons aimed at Wintner. That was the key. So long as the General was convinced that Wintner valued his own life, then the General thought he had an advantage. *Of course* Wintner wouldn't try to trick him. The General would kill him if he tried anything. And Wintner wouldn't want that, would he?

Wintner's use of the code phrase "Bamse bomb" had told his ship's armourers exactly what to do. He had asked the General if there was any place in particular he wanted the bomb delivered, a weapons depot, perhaps, or missile facility.

The General had requested this courtyard 200 meters from the caves. Undoubtedly this was so he could make a spectacle of the event. But Wintner wondered if they even had facilities. Once they got the weapon, how did they plan to deliver it? Did they have missiles? Were they going to use a boat?

Ejar said, "If anything other than a weapons shipment comes out of that little ship–a security squad, perhaps–my people will kill you and the squad." He gestured towards the crowd. "Nearly everyone here is a civilian, but even Troth civilians carry blasters."

"No soldiers are coming," said Wintner. He hoped the Troth weren't too trigger-happy. Ejar wouldn't exactly be getting what he expected.

The repulse jets from the plane fired and the boxy craft with stubby wings settled in the center of the courtyard.

The back hatch slowly lowered, and a large crate rolled out to the center of the courtyard. Like everyone else facing the plane, Wintner looked inside. There was no pilot. The flight down had been controlled from his command ship. Good.

"Your bomb," said Wintner.

The four sides of the crate popped off. The object that sat inside was about two meters tall, shiny, cylindrical, and had five claw-like feet sprouting around its base.

Suddenly, the five feet quickly dug themselves through the base of the crate and into the stone floor of the courtyard, clearly implanting the cylinder in the ground. The sound of metal on stone–or rather, *in* stone–and the sudden silence when the operation ended announced to everyone present that the cylinder was now firmly moored.

Ejar spun around and aimed his blaster at Wintner.

"One thermonuclear device, General," said Wintner.

"I ought to kill you now."

But you haven't, thought Wintner. *And you won't. You need answers first. It may already be too late for you to act irresponsibly.*

"I would advise you, General, not to attempt to move or disable the device. It's a crude fission weapon and any tampering with it may cause it to detonate. This nuclear bomb is now part of Troth. We have given the detonation device to the First Speaker of the Cintro council. If any nation harms any other nation–not just Cintro–Troth will be destroyed."

"What!"

"Congratulations, General," said Wintner, "you are now the most powerful man on the planet. You are now the head of a planet-wide police force." The General stared at Wintner. "Troth is now Menim's police force. It's time you turned your nation's considerable talents for espionage and destruction, as well as your obvious resourcefulness, toward protecting your world."

"You wouldn't dare!"

"It's not up to me, General. The control device is in the hands of the Cintro government. You tell me: Would *they* dare?"

"You cannot countenance the destruction of a nation. What about the environmental hazards? Fallout!"

"Luckily, you are already an island, so that is not much of a danger."

"This is—ahhhh!" Ejar laughed. "Ah, Ambassador, you almost had me. But I am not the Blind Man of Pasa. This is not a weapon after all, is it? No, of course not. The great Coalition would not do that."

"Yes," said Wintner. "It is real. I assume you have scanners."

General Ejar gestured to one of soldiers who approached the anchored cylinder with some sort of wand. He pointed it at the device from a respectful distance then, looking at a tiny green screen on the wand, nodded to Ejar.

"May Sabu take your eyes, Wintner! It will never be absolute peace. How can one nation...I mean, a whole planet!"

The Ambassador said, "Increased and more civil communication between Troth and Cintro would probably decrease the odds of a detonation due to simple misunderstandings. I would begin there."

"This is completely unacceptable!" yelled the General. Several of his soldiers approached Wintner, raising their weapons. "That we should be punished for the actions of any other nation-state, like Uru or Saund."

Now was the time to fake unflappability.

The Ambassador smiled. "General, the Troth have shown

resourcefulness, aggression, and imagination. All the elements necessary to become the planet's police. You have been able to assassinate Cintro leaders, destroy its most valued cultural treasures, and disrupt commerce. Imagine what you could do if turned your forces and energies to preventing destruction and violence?" Wintner stepped forward and looked into Ejar's eyes. "And you have the ultimate motivation to do so."

"Blackmail," said the General, his voice filled with loathing. "I demand—"

"You are not in a position to demand anything. You are only in a position to get to work. Cintro, on the other hand, is in a position to enforce everything."

"And they would do it too. All for the sake of unifying us and joining your ridiculous Coalition."

"I hope so," said Wintner. He turned and began walking towards the astroplane. "We will be in touch," he said. He walked forward slowly. If they didn't fire…If he made it to the plane…

He climbed the ramp, and it rose behind him.

Sitting down in the pilot's seat, Wintner breathed for the first time in what seemed like an hour. He engaged the engine and smiled. Self-interest; the greatest force for peace in the universe. The Coalition was built on it.

~*~

The Off World Kick Murder Squad

Daniel Arthur Smith

~*~

I've been to the farthest points of the colonies, shiny and shamble, and I tell ya, you can travel through a tube that puts you five Planes deep or a thousand light years out and I don't care if it's a Bureau Station, Syndicate City, or some mining rock floating in the belt, the first watering hole you'll step into will have stained, black carpet walls lit by some sad shade of behind-the-bar-dim neon and the perpetual disinfectant scent hanging in the air from the last jackass-turned-genius they had to clean up for shooting his mouth off.

When Hodge and I walked into the Teller Free-Port dive, it was no different; the chemical trace was thick enough to burn your nose up to the underside of your eye sockets. I could've guessed where that old courier would be waiting for us, even if Cassidy hadn't given me a heads-up. He was planted in the back-corner booth, as predictable as a seven on a Stilson die, behind a pole dancer wearing nothing but a thin coat of body paint the same depressing blue that dreamcast out from the bar.

Hodge waited sentinel near the door while I moved in for the meet.

Slayden had one of those digital ink masks you see on the anarchs and some of the mercs, the kind of mask my team paints on to befuddle the facial recognition systems, only permanent. The neon shadowed his indigo tatt in a way that made the thin man's cheeks appear hollow, made him look gaunter than he naturally was, practically a skull. Couriers usually wore a shimmer at best—apparel mods like a collar pin or a tie clip that merely altered their appearance. But he was going for some kind of grim, ominous look and relished it.

Slayden was no average courier, and meeting with him meant this was to be no average job.

He didn't look at me when I approached; instead, he kept a lascivious focus on the naked writhing body in front of his table. What he did do was extend a lanky hand in my direction and gesture for me to sit next to him on the booth. All but a few humans have an age mod, and I figured Slayden had one too. But even behind the tatt I could see the tight wrinkles of a man near sixty, which only meant his was put in a long time ago, when the technology was new. Word was that Slayden had been around during the Plane wars of Alpha Earth, that he was a bureaucrat that mobbed up. None of it mattered to me. I was looking for our next payday, and a meeting with Slayden was as good as a job from any other. With a deep hiss—another hint of his age—he flatly said, "The device is being loaded onto your ship." He wheezed out his words from lungs that had been too abused and scarred for any mod to heal. His tone went well with his apocalyptic get up, but it added to my distrust of the man. I kept my cards tight.

"So where do we need to deliver this—device?" I asked.

"You don't need to deliver anything. It will deliver you."

"Hold on," I said. "Letcher didn't say anything about jumping Planes. I don't even want a quant near my ship. You tell him the deal's off."

"Relax, my old friend. Everyone in the quadrant knows you'll travel anywhere to get the job done. That's why we call on you, you're the best kick murder squad across the known Planes…" he picked up the clear glass of liquor in front of him. "And it's not even a quantum device." He took slow draw from his drink. "Not really."

"What's that supposed to mean?"

Slayden reached into his shirt pocket, withdrew a small clear card, and, with eyes still fixed on the painted dancer, passed it to me. With my forefinger, I traced an inverted 'V' and cyclone of red numbers appeared in the V's place. They spun for a brief second and then flew across the surface, forming the image of a star map and the aligned coordinates.

"You have to be kidding," I said.

"You've infiltrated Syndicate before."

"The least of my concerns." I slid the card into my own pocket. "You sure this is for real?"

"And so is the fee."

I signaled Hodge that we were on. He acknowledged with a slight tilt of his head. When he did, the iridescence of his too blue eyes briefly lit brightly and then softened again. I darted my own eyes over to Cassidy at the bar, scantily clad, fondling the arm of the station agent. She was three drinks in with him, hadn't left his side since we docked. I guess she saw the gesture because she whispered something into the agent's ear and, when he flagged the bartender, she excused herself.

"Okay then," I said as I stood. "Consider it done."

"We already have," said Slayden, his voice breathy, revolting.

Then I added, "For another twenty-percent." It wasn't so much about the quant–though that was a fifty-fifty death trap in and of itself–or that we were infiltrating Syndicate. If the job wasn't dangerous, Letcher wouldn't be hiring us. No, I upped the fee because I don't much care for Slayden.

"Twenty? It's already a double fee."

"You said it yourself, we're the best."

"Okay. Done," he said. He didn't hesitate with his dismissive response, but I knew I'd managed to scratch him where he didn't want.

I turned away, but Slayden added, "You know there's another reason we call on you."

"And why is that?" I asked without facing him.

"Because we don't have to worry about you ever betraying us. The whole 'shoot on sight' thing."

I wanted to smirk and speak my mind, maybe give Slayden a new scar to go with his face tatt, but I didn't want to give him the benefit of a reaction. So, I just said, "Are we done?"

"Be safe," he said, his focus on the dancer, who was now bouncing her ass at him. She winked at me as I passed. I gave her a grin and crossed to the door. Hodge fell in behind me.

The bright light of the promenade was a stark contrast to the inside of the bar. But our eyes didn't need to adjust. Not because they had mods—they did—but because we were entirely Synthetic ourselves. Our entire team was. Synthetic the same way the giraffes and elephants were back on Alpha, except we were Mortal Syns to the last. And what Slayden said about 'shoot on sight,' there was truth to that. Assassination wasn't our only business, but twenty-three dead humans and a stolen transport had sealed our fate, and what we had to say about it didn't matter. From then on out, we were a kick murder squad. That old sly mobster bringing up Layton Four didn't make me feel too easy.

I was putting my steps forward with a purpose, Hodge walked the same, thumbs on our sabers, ready to draw. But there was no need. I shifted my jaw to engage my chin chip—the splinter of tech in the center of my chin that amplifies my mandible—and then spoke in a whisper. "Anson, are we good to go?"

Anson was quick to answer. "She's loaded and ready," he said. "And I installed the new crystal set I picked up for the aft panel."

"Okay. Good. I want everybody to wrap it up and get back to the ship. Bailer?"

"Already on my way," said Bailer.

"Did you get us a good haul?"

"You bet. If I'd 've stayed in the casino any longer, they'd 've shot me."

"Will?"

"The trade was harsh," Will responded, "but I have the med tech I was looking for."

"Did they ask any questions?"

"Not for what I paid them. I couldn't get the Telinium, though. We'll have to find some soon."

I heard what Will said but the laughter of a group of children running through the crowd triggered an alert to my right peripheral. The deck rats raced and dodged among the less experienced travelers in a faux game of tag, inviting curses as they knocked the rich, the naïve, and the gravity sick aside. "Watch out!" exclaimed an Arcadian woman as two of the children pulled at the sides of her aubergine robes. "You'll rip my gown," she said. Arcadians rarely left their Plane and never mingled with the likes of common people. I figured her greatest concern was that the riff raff of the station might contaminate her somehow. Little did she know, the pigtailed ginger and her dark-skinned friend were fleecing any valuables they could slide their limber fingers onto. I scanned past the crowing woman and into the crowd of the promenade. Green augments outlined the other travelers and traders traversing the market stalls. Green was good. There were no threats.

There was a memory.

A moment where I thought I could've been on Rasa Four. One station's promenade looks like the other. Teller Free-Port was of the common Hauser design; essentially a long cylindrical operations core with a wide habitat disc in her center and six outer rings—terminals to the landing bays—smaller on the outreached ends, larger towards the station's center, giving Teller the appearance of two cones placed together at their base.

We exited the promenade at the Delta Ring gate, no elevator, rather one of four spoked corridors extending out to the terminal.

Will spoke again. "Would you like me to keep looking?"

"Looking?" I asked.

"For the Telinium."

"No," I said. "Whatever you have is good. Just get back to the ship."

"Is something up?" asked Bailer.

Bailer's psychology enhancements were a sixth sense benefit to the team, particularly in the casino, but I wasn't fond of his pinpoint detection when it came to me. Still, there was no point avoiding the question. "Something was said that rubbed me the wrong way," I said. "I'll feel a ton better when we're off this station."

"Gotcha," Bailer replied.

As we reached the Delta-Gamma bay, I heard the soft slap of mag boots approaching from the other end of the curved corridor. It was Bailer. Hodge and I didn't wait for him; instead, we punched the code to open the doors and went inside. Teller was large for a Free-Port Station, and so were her loading bays; three m-class transports including our own sat near the wide-open launch bay window. Cassidy and Anson stood at the gangway, the fuchsia cloud of the Monrovian gas cluster painting the stars behind them. The dock was stacked with sealed storage crates, most waiting for ships yet to arrive, others stocked with goods for the station. The two other transports parked either side of the chromium Jentu were dark, had been when the team arrived. The bay door opened at my back; that was Bailer.

Hodge and I joined Cassidy and Anson beneath the delta wing of the Jentu.

"Where are the twins?" I asked.

"Inside," said Anson.

Cassidy looked past my shoulder. "Did you get it?" she asked Bailer.

Bailer crossed his arms to reach into either side of his jacket and then pulled out two brown bottles. "Not just one, but two," he said. A tooth-filled grin covered his face.

Cassidy went right to him, taking one of the bottles from his hands. "You devil," she said. "How did you pull that off?" She reached for the other and Bailer pulled it away before she could take hold of it.

"Remember what you promised," said Bailer.

"For two of these, I'll do your laundry for a month," she said. She twisted off the top of the bottle she held and sniffed the contents. "Genuine."

"What is it?" asked Hodge. "And how come he has none for me?"

"I don't think you'd want it," said Anson.

"How'd you know I don't want any?"

"Because it's Lometra."

"What's that?"

I added, "It's squeezed from scent gland of the flying eel."

Hodge knotted his face in disgust. "Whut? Bolts? I hate those things. A swarm hit me on Entaur." He held up his scarred forearm. "Bit right through my suit, almost killed me from exposure." He shirked his upper body. "Why she want somethin out of an eel ass anyway?"

"It's a perfume," I said.

"She puts that on her?"

"It's very special," said Cassidy.

"What's so special about it?" Hodge asked, so she held the bottle toward him. "Get that away from me," he said. But then he caught a whiff. "Hey, that's nice."

Cassidy rolled her eyes away. "See? I told you."

"That's real nice," Hodge added as Cassidy looped her arm around Anson.

"Down boy," said Anson. Then he kissed Cassidy.

The bay doors opened again. Will entered the dock with the medical goods he'd traded for slung over his shoulder in a huge black pack to haul. We may be synthetic but we're not invincible.

"Good," I said. "That's all of us. Hodge, circle around with Anson for the final check. Then we can get on our way."

"Aye, aye," said Hodge as he and Anson split off to inspect the bottom of the Jentu hull.

Will was almost to us when the bay doors opened again. Will had been smiling, but when he heard the whoosh of the doors, his face went plain. Either he'd suspected who was following him or he saw that the rest of us were already inside and instinctually reacted to the sound of the door at his back. Living on the run makes for a hair trigger reaction. He looked into my eyes, swung his neck around to see who was at the door, and then met my eyes again with a sense of urgency that told me the three entering were more than trouble. Of course, we all figured that right fast ourselves. Two of the three were Bureau Boys and they had orders to shoot on sight. The third man wore a med tunic. probably one of the pharmacists that traded with Will. The doors weren't even fully opened when the man's arm shot out towards us. "There. That's him. I told you, and look there, that's Eller and the whole bunch."

~*~

Hearing my name was the worst of signs. Hodge and I both drew sabers. But the Bureau Boys drew guns, and not even station safe concussion blasters. No, they drew proper ordinance blasting assault weapons from their hips.

It would've been a beauty if we could've just ran up into the ship, but the blaster fire separated us from the hatch. We dodged, best we could, behind whatever was the closest. Hodge and I made it behind one stack of crates, Cassidy, Anson, and Bailer, another. Will made a run for it but couldn't dive fast enough. A blaster blew a large hole clear through his middle. He collapsed on the end of the gangway. From where the rest of us watched, pinned down, I could see the last spark of life leave him. His eyes flared bright blue and then darkened. As soon as Will's face lost life, Hodge's took on the rage of the fight.

"Forget this," he said. "They ain't putting no hole in me unless it's a fair fight." He raised his saber above us and swung it down toward the Jentu. I didn't know why he was swinging at open air, but he saw something to the side that I hadn't seen before. The Bureau Boys fired on his saber following it down as he swung. They didn't hit it, of course, but they hit right where Hodge wanted them to. The energy shells pummeled a crate. The devil lit Hodge's face and I caught on to what he was doing. The crate was labeled with a munitions icon. Hodge shoved his saber out again and the Bureau Boys fired again. This time busting the side of the crate open.

There inside was a standing rack of long guns. The problem was that they were exposed to the men firing at us. Hodge's lower jaw slid forward, setting aim for what he was about to do.

"Here goes nothing," he said, and then he rolled toward the long guns, grabbed one, and kept rolling for the cover of the crate on the other side. The Bureau Boys sent over a burst, but he took them by surprise and they were too slow with their aim.

"Hooeee!!" hollered Hodge, already fixing the weapon to shoot. He hit charge, and the long gun emitted a high-pitched whir. It escalated to a climax—and then began to quiet. Hodge slammed the power cartridge with the palm of his hand, once, twice, and then a third time. With disbelief, he looked over at me and yelled, "It's reading empty."

At the bottom of the broken crate was a case of power cartridges. I dove, grabbed, and rolled. I felt the heat of the bursts flying past me, and nearly lost my leg when one of the long guns blew. From the deck, I handed Hodge a cartridge. His long gun began whirring again, this time hitting full pitch before quieting. In one fluid motion, Hodge raised the barrel of the long gun over the top of the crate and let loose a rapid volley toward the Bureau Boys.

The three attackers hadn't even taken cover.

Those Bureau Boys surely had the best of legal mods, but Hodge was built for this.

The man who brought the Bureau Boys in had stepped behind the two, but as he was dead center, Hodge freed him of his head. The Bureau Boys jumped to either side, seeking cover.

"Run," I yelled.

I saw Rhea inside the hatch, waving us in. One by one, the team made for the gangway. Each time one of the Bureau Boys even raised his weapon, Hodge would fire first. Bailer made it into the Jentu, followed by Cassidy. She grabbed Will's bag from his limp arm, energy shells surging a breath above her. There was a brief moment she paused, set on Will, maybe deciding if he might still have a chance. Then she went for the hatch and Bailer and Rhea's waiting arms. Then it was Anson's turn. He darted toward the hatch, but the Bureau Boys had already made up for their mistake and were firing simultaneous and blind. They missed Anson directly but blew up another crate, sending debris into his side.

With Anson sitting out in the open, there was no time to hesitate. The Bureau Boys couldn't lock on, but all they needed was one lucky shot and they'd have another of our fast dwindling crew. I slapped Hodge on the back and gave him a tug as I launched toward Anson. Hodge squeezed the trigger of the long gun and ran as a shield as I raked up Anson. Rhea already had the hatch shutting as we made it inside.

"Get him below deck!" I yelled as made for the bridge.

There was no time to waste clearing the station. If I commed in, it would've merely been a heads-up for someone to start shooting. So, I rapidly set the controls and leaned into the stick.

"How long you figure we have before those fellas get to their ship?" Bailer asked from the second chair.

"Not long enough," I said, peeking out for any ship that may be guarding the bay.

"You think there are more of them?" he asked. He too was leaning forward and searching the outside of the station.

"Now how would I know that? There weren't supposed to be any Bureau on Teller in the first place."

"Right," he said. "Well, they travel in pairs. If there was a fleet ship nearby, we'd know."

I pulled the card Slayden had given me from my pocket. That's when I realized my hands and front were doused in blood. I wiped my fingers across the side of my hip and then drew the 'V' icon on the card. The red vortex reappeared and coordinates illuminated the small screen.

"We have to get that device online," I said and keyed in the linking codes.

"What device?" Bailer asked.

"The one that's going to shift us out of here."

"There's a quant onboard? Letcher didn't say anything about a quant."

"Slayden said it's something different."

"Call it what you want. Hodge isn't going to take too kindly to having a quant on board."

The device's prompts filled the screen. "Well, it's here. And I don't think we have time to wait." I gestured to a screen that showed our five. A Bureau Fleet corvette was creeping around from the starboard side of the Jentu.

"How'd they get out there so fast?"

"That's not them, it's too big."

"They only travel in pairs, and we're too far out for a warship that small. I mean, what's a Homeland patrol doing this far out anyway?"

"All good points," I said as I entered the coordinates from the card, "and we'll discuss them at a later time."

"Hey, I recognize those coordinates. We can't go there."

"Now's not the time. As soon as they clear the station, they'll be able to fire on us."

A hail came over the Jentu's bridge speakers. "Attention, Attention. Captain of the Jentu class vessel. This is the Cobalt. In the name of the Homeland, return to dock. Return to dock or we will be forced to fire."

"Turn that off," I said. "They're just waiting for a clear shot."

As Bailer shut down the outside channel he said, "To hell with those coordinates. We can still outrun them."

"Maybe we could, maybe we couldn't, but that ship is a missile carrier. Probably phase shifters. And we can't outrun or out-maneuver ordinance like that out here in the open. I'm not Anson."

"We don't know if they're Phase shifters."

"No, we don't. Another good point to discuss later. That's it. The device will initiate in twenty, nineteen…

"Eight—"

Bailer lunged in front of me, onto the console. "I can't let you do that!" he yelled.

His torso was in my chest. I grabbed at his arm to shove him aside. "Have you lost it?"

"If we go there, we die," he said, pushing his weight against me.

"You don't know that," I said, giving him another shove, this time pushing him away. He moved back in, but not before I was able to rise and block him. "Stand down," I said, "or you're going to get us all killed."

Bailer smirked, said, "Sorry captain," and brought his right shoulder back to strike me. I blocked the punch with my left and throat punched him with my right.

He stumbled backward, both hands to his throat.

"Not as sorry as me," I said.

His eyes went fierce and his hands dropped from his throat as he made yet another run for me. A concussion blast across our bow shook the bridge and caused him to lose his footing and stumble to a knee. Behind him, the twins were entering the bridge.

"Will you restrain him please?" I said to the two and, without question, one took either side, pinning him to the floor.

I jumped back into the pilot seat and looked at the screen to a two... one.

~*~

ABOUT THE AUTHORS

Nathan M. Beauchamp started writing stories at nine years old and never stopped. From his first grisly tales about carnivorous catfish, mole detectives, and cyborg housecats, his interests have always delved into strange waters. Nathan works in finance so that he can support his habit of putting words together in the hope that someone will read them. His hobbies include reading, photography, arguing for sport, and pondering the eventual heat death of the universe. He has published many short stories in magazines and anthologies, and holds an MFA in creative writing from Western State. He lives in Colorado with his wife and two young boys.

Nathan co-created the award winning YA science fiction series **Universe Eventual** where he writes as N.J. Tanger. The series includes *Chimera*, *Helios*, and *Ceres* and the prequel *Ascension*. **Universe Eventual** is available on Amazon.

For more information, visit njtanger.com

Samuel Peralta is a physicist and storyteller. An Amazon bestselling author, he is also the creator of the acclaimed *Future Chronicles* series, with 17 consecutive titles ranking at the top of the Amazon Bestselling Anthology lists, many hitting the mainstream Top 10 Bestsellers list. His own work has been named in *Best American Science Fiction and Fantasy*.

His poetry has ranked #1 on Amazon, Goodreads, Twitter, and has been spotlighted in articles on *Best American Poetry*. Awards include from the BBC, the Digital Literature Institute, and the Palanca Memorial Awards for Literature.

An award-winning PhD, he's designed nuclear robotic tools and co-founded several software and semiconductor start-ups. He is also a producer and ardent supporter of independent film.

For more information, visit www.smarturl.it/get-free-book

A.K. Meek A mild-mannered management engineer by day, a mild-mannered writer by night, Anthony writes speculative, slipstream science fiction and fantasy. He has penned alternate realities where robots are treated as gods fallen to earth, built cities filled to the brim with artificial animals, and crafted stories of alien invaders that can see human thought. He has also dipped his hand in "Jericho" style post-apocalyptic fiction and birthed a fantastic world where truth and lie can occupy the same space. He lives in the Deep South, among the mosquitoes and magnolias, with his wonderful wife and menagerie of dogs and cats, and a wild rabbit that occasionally strays into the back yard for a visit.

For more information, visit akmeek.com

Kevin Lauderdale has written essays and articles for the *Los Angeles Times*, *The Dictionary of American Biography*, and *McSweeneys.net*. His short fiction has appeared in several of Pocket Books' *Star Trek* anthologies as well as various small press publications. This story was originally published in *Cthulhu Unbound* in 2009. It made Ellen Datlow's Honorable Mention list for that year's best horror and was nominated for a Washington Area Science Fiction Association Small Press Award for Best Short Story. A sequel, "James and the Prince of Darkness," can be found in the 2015 anthology *Ain't Superstitious*, from Third Flatiron Publishing. With Jeff Ayers, he has written *The Fourth Lion*, a YA thriller set in contemporary Washington, D.C. and its surroundings. He hosts the Old Time Radio podcast, *"Presenting the Transcription Feature,"* and co-hosts *"Temple of Bad,"* the podcast about movies that are so bad, they're practically a religious experience, both on the Chronic Rift network. He is a member of SFWA and HWA.

For more information, visit
kevinlauderdale.livejournal.com

Daniel Arthur Smith is the author of the international bestsellers *Hugh Howey Lives*, *The Cathari Treasure*, *The Somali Deception*, and a few other novels and short stories. He also curates the phenomenal short fiction series *Tales from the Canyons of the Damned*.

He was raised in Michigan and graduated from Western Michigan University where he studied philosophy, with focus on cognitive science, meta-physics, and comparative religion. He began his career as a bartender, barista, poetry house proprietor, teacher, and then became a technologist and futurist for the Fortune 100 across the Americas and Europe.

Daniel has traveled to over 300 cities in 22 countries, residing in Los Angeles, Kalamazoo, Prague, Crete, and now writes in Manhattan where he lives with his wife and young sons.

For more information, visit danielarthursmith.com

~*~

Made in the USA
San Bernardino, CA
24 December 2016